BAD FOOD

Live and Let Fry

By Eric Luper

Illustrated by
"The Doodle Boy" Joe Whale

Scholastic Inc.

ISBN 978-1-339-04508-5

10 9 8 7 6 5 4 3 2 1   23 24 25 26 27

Printed in China   68

First printing 2023

Book design by Katie Fitch

SCHOOL MAP

CHAPTER 1

Letting Off Steam

As always, night had come to Belching Walrus Elementary. The doors were locked, the hallways were silent, and the intercom didn't let out a crackle. Oh, and everyone in the cafeteria was letting off steam.

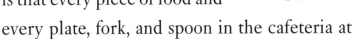

No, what I meant to say is that every piece of food and every plate, fork, and spoon in the cafeteria at

Belching Walrus Elementary come alive each night to have fun. Every night.

And ever since the folks from the other rooms in the school helped Slice, Scoop, and Totz stop the sneaky Class Pets from setting their traps . . .

Well, it's all been pretty good since then.

And, as always, best friends forever Slice (a brave and cheesy slice of pizza), Scoop (a triple

scoop ice cream cone—vanilla, chocolate, AND strawberry), and Totz (a crunchy, delicious, and trendy tater tot) were blowing off their own steam under the utility sink.

"Hey, where's Totz?" Slice said.

Scoop looked up from the painting she was working on. "I don't know," she said. "I've been too busy working on my newest creation."

She spun her canvas around. The painting was divided into four squares: one blue, one yellow, one green, and one pink. Each square had a painting of Scoop in it.

"It's a self-portrait," Scoop said.

Slice flexed his arms to make tiny muscles. "Wouldn't you rather paint a picture of me?"

Scoop laughed. "A self-portrait is more than just a picture," she said. "It shows how the artist sees themself."

Slice looked at the painting again. "So, you see yourself in four colored squares?"

Scoop rolled her eyes.

Just then, they heard a grunt. Totz was hanging upside down from a string above them.

"What are you doing?" Slice asked.

"Shhh . . . Act natural," Totz said. "I'm being a spy."

"How long have you been hanging up there?" Scoop asked.

"Too . . . long." Totz grunted.

Suddenly, the string let go and Totz fell.

He sprang to his feet and straightened his headphones. "I told you to hold on to that string until I tugged three times," Totz called out, looking up.

Their egg friends, Sal and Monella, poked their faces over the edge of the sink.

"You're too heavy for our little hands," Sal said.

"Plus, we're late for our daily speed walk," Monella added.

And with that, Sal and Monella disappeared. Slice, Scoop, and Totz could hear them as they went off.

Left, right, left, right, left, right . . .

"Hey, nice self-portrait," Totz said. "It shows the many sides of you—similar but also different."

Scoop smiled and then glared at Slice. "At least someone gets me."

"So why do you want to be a spy?" Slice asked Totz.

"Now that I've learned to play the banjo, I need a new hobby," he explained. "I thought being a spy would be fun and interesting."

"What do you know about being a spy?" Slice asked.

"Plenty," Totz said, leaning against a box none of them had ever seen before. "We are always sneaking around and solving problems. Our friend Rasher can make gadgets. And I already have the sunglasses."

"Have you learned any spy skills?" Scoop said.

"Like what?" Totz asked.

"Like problem-solving," Slice said.

"Being a master of disguise," Scoop said.

"And blending in with other cultures," Slice said.

"Yup," Totz said. "I can do all those things."

Slice shrugged. "Then I guess you're on your way to being a spy."

Just then, a thump came from inside a cardboard box none of them had ever seen before.

"Stand aside," a voice said. "Coming through."

It was Glizzy the hot dog. He came running over with Sprinkles the donut, who (as always) was trailing sprinkles behind her. Glizzy pressed his ear to the side of the box.

"Hello?!?" he called out. He knocked on the box and said it again. "Hello?!?"

Muffled voices came from inside.

Glizzy and Sprinkles placed their hands on the side of the box and pushed. It didn't budge.

"Slice, Scoop, Totz, can you please help us?" Sprinkles said.

The group rocked the box back and forth. Finally, it tipped over and the lid popped open.

Out marched dozens of donuts. Some were round with a hole in the middle, some were long and twisty, and some were stuffed on the inside. Some were glazed, some were frosted, some had sprinkles, and some had nothing at all. There were pink donuts, chocolate donuts, and a few that looked as though their sprinkles were baked right inside.

The largest of these donuts, a round fellow wearing an eyepatch, waddled out. He had short arms and legs and a perfect coating of purple frosting. Alongside him walked a much smaller, plain donut.

"My name is Captain Donut," the largest donut proclaimed. "I am the captain of the Mobile Donut Command Center. This is my son, Fry. You are all in great danger. We are here to help."

"Morty!" Sprinkles called out. She threw her arms around Captain Donut.

"Hi, Sprinkles," Captain Donut said. "It's been so long. But when I'm on a mission, please don't call me Morty. Call me Captain Donut."

"Oh, look who's so fancy all of a sudden," Sprinkles said.

Captain Donut went on, "As I was saying, there is a great danger lurking. We are here to help."

CHAPTER 1A

Oopsies!

Wait a second.

Before we go any further, we almost forgot one important thing . . .

Character bios.

What would our book series be without a few character bios?

So here goes . . .

Name: Rasher

Food Type: Piece of bacon

Personality: Loud and friendly

Strengths: Brilliant inventor, smells delicious

Weakness: Smells so delicious people can't resist him!

Fears: Large crowds

Hobby: Inventing things

Name: Richard

Type: Book (subtype: dictionary)

Personality: Serious and gruff, yells sometimes

Strength: Knows the meaning of every word there is

Weaknesses: A little bossy and very slow

Fears: Fire, water, being mis-shelved!

Hobby: Spelling bees (undefeated)

Name: Captain Morty Leopold Donut III

Type: Donut (purple frosted)

Personality: Always professional and official

Strength: Born leader

Weakness: Maybe a little *too* official

Fears: Unknown

Interesting Fact: Lost his eye because someone tested his freshness.

Now back to our story . . .

CHAPTER 2

A Great Danger Lurking

By now, most of the residents of the Cafeteria had gathered around. After all, it wasn't every day that donuts marched out of a cardboard box to warn of a great danger lurking.

Sprinkles cried rainbow sprinkles of joy. "Morty," she sobbed. "It's been so long!"

"You know each other?" Scoop asked.

"Of course," Sprinkles told her. "Morty and I came from the same bakery. That makes us family."

Captain Donut walked over to them. "There is a great danger lurking underneath Belching Walrus Elementary," he said.

"Is the danger a belching walrus?" Slice asked.

Fry busted out laughing.

Captain Donut frowned. "This is nothing to laugh about, Fry."

"What sort of danger?" Glizzy asked.

"Join me in our Mobile Donut Command Center," Captain Donut said. He led them into the cardboard box. It was no ordinary

THIS IS NO ORDINARY CARDBOARD BOX...

cardboard box.

On the outside, the cardboard box looked like any other—brown, box shaped, and slightly frayed around the edges. But on the inside, the cardboard box was lined wall-to-wall with fancy chairs, computer monitors, and blinking lights.

"Welcome to the Mobile Donut Command Center," Captain Donut said. "From here, we can keep track of everything going on at Belching Walrus Elementary."

They looked at the monitors. Each one showed a different part of the school. One showed Coach and his sports equipment playing kickball in the Gym. Another showed Baron von Lineal barking orders to the highlighters in the Main Office. A third showed the Class Pets wrestling in the Science Room. Other monitors showed different rooms in Belching Walrus Elementary, but you get the idea.

"You're spying on us," Scoop said. "Isn't that kind of wrong?"

"The better we can see you, the better we can protect you," Captain Donut said.

"So, where were you when Baron von Lineal from the Main Office tried to take over the Cooler?" Totz said.

"Where were you when the aliens Gleb and Lauren tried to steal all the mustard packets from the Pantry and take them to outer space?" Slice asked.

"Where were you when the Class Pets from the Science Room tried to use us as bait to catch a crazed ferret on the loose?" Scoop asked.

Captain Donut shook his purple-frosted head. "All minor issues," he said. "Betty's Bakery only sends the Mobile Donut Command Center when things get *really* dangerous."

"Like now," Fry added.

"Mouth closed, eyes open," Captain Donut said to Fry. "Someday, you will wear your own purple frosting and command your own Mobile Donut Command Center."

Fry tugged on his father's arm. "But what if I don't want to have purple frosting and command my own Mobile Donut Command Center?"

Captain Donut knelt. "And what would you like to do?"

Fry puffed out his chest. "I want to wear white frosting with red sprinkles and be a medic!"

Sprinkles gasped. "And get jelly and Boston cream all over yourself every day?"

"I want to help donuts of all shapes and sizes, from the tiniest donut hole to the biggest apple fritter," Fry said.

"Nonsense," Captain Donut said. "Our family comes from a long line of purple-frosted Mobile Donut Command Center commanders. Your grandmother and grandfather, your great-grandmother and your great-great-grandpappy Erastus O. McCruller. You don't want to let them all down, do you?"

Fry looked disappointed and shrugged. "I guess not."

"Now, to catch you all up," Captain Donut said. "Our secret agent Strawberry

Surprise sent a message from Sub-Basement 3 of Belching Walrus Elementary. I'd like you to have a look."

Captain Donut directed their attention to the largest monitor in the command center. The video was blurry and dark. The sound was broken up with static.

"If anyone gets this message"—crackle—"send backup," Strawberry Surprise said. "Just as . . . we . . . suspected"—crackle—"the threat . . . real"—crackle—"Mus Musculus . . . invaded"—crackle—"Coming your w—"

The video cut out.

"It's all we have," Captain Donut said.

"What's a Muck Muckulus?" Totz asked.

"She said Mus Musculus," Captain Donut said. "We have no idea what that is."

Scoop looked closely at the monitor. "Strawberry Surprise is in trouble," she said.

"We need to save her," Slice added.

"We're already on it," Captain Donut said. He pressed a few buttons, and the monitors lit up, each one showing the face of a different donut. "Cruller Team 7, are you ready?"

One of the long, slender donuts on the monitors replied, "We're in position."

"Ready as a twice-baked potato," another donut said.

"Piece of cake," another voice added.

The video was fuzzy, but they could see Cruller Team 7 walking down a long hallway. Suddenly, one of the monitors went black. Then another.

"McIntyre," one of the soldiers said. "Where'd ya go?"

"They're all around us!" another said.

There was a puff of powdered sugar, and another monitor went black. Then another.

"Get them out of there," Glizzy said. "They're getting sautéed!"

Three more monitors went black.

Captain Donut grabbed the microphone. "Pull out," he yelled. "Withdraw! Withdraw!"

"There's too many of them," a voice said. "There's no way out!"

Slice, Scoop, and Totz watched in horror as the last of the monitors went black.

Captain Donut dropped his head. "They were our best hope," he said.

Glizzy and Sprinkles gathered around Captain Donut. Glizzy patted him on the back. "You did your best," Glizzy said.

"Maybe we should just stay out of Sub-Basement 3," Totz suggested.

Just then, one of the monitors crackled and the camera went back on.

"We're coming for *you* next," a screechy voice said. "No one at Belching Walrus Elementary is safe. Nom, nom, nom."

"Who are you? What do you want?" Captain Donut asked.

"I am Mus Musculus, leader of F.E.A.R.S.O.M.E. Deliver all your crackers to us and no further harm will come to you."

"And cheese," another voice said.

"Yes, and cheese," Mus Musculus said.

"Camembert, Gorgonzola, and Limburger . . . The stinkier the better."

"We do not listen to threats," Captain Donut said.

"Then perhaps you will listen to this . . ." Mus Musculus said. "It is eight o'clock now. If we do not receive our crackers and stinky cheese by midnight, we will cut the power to the whole school. That means no Cooler, no lights, no computers, no electric pencil sharpeners.

"You have four hours," the voice said. The monitor cut out.

Slice glanced at Scoop and Totz. "We've got to do something," he said.

"I'm coming with you," Fry said.

Scoop shook her chocolate-vanilla-and-strawberry head. "No, you're not," she said. "It's too dangerous, and you're too little."

"Sometimes little can be good," Fry said.

"We're *all* too little," Totz said. "You saw what happened to Cruller Team 7. We won't last five seconds down there."

"We might not last five seconds down there *by ourselves*," Slice said. "But I know someone who can help."

CHAPTER 3
Someone Who Can Help

Slice, **Scoop, Totz,** and Fry entered the Cooler. They weaved through a maze of boxes. They climbed over several pipes and scooted under a few more. Scoop pushed aside a case of frozen hamburger patties and knocked on the wall.

A muffled voice sounded from the other side. "What's the password?"

Slice looked at his friends and shrugged. "Crab mofongo?" he guessed.

"Incorrect," the voice said.

"Bangers and mash?" Scoop said.

"Wrong again," the voice said.

"Lopadotemachoselachogaleokrani-oleipsanodrimhypotrimmatosilphioparaomeli-tokatakechymenokichlepikossyphophattoperi-steralektryonoptekephalliokigklopeleiolagoio-siraiobaphetraganopterygon," Totz said.

A hidden door popped open, and Rasher poked his head out. The scent of salty

BOILING BANANAS!

deliciousness floated out. "Boiling bananas, how did you know the password was lopad-otemachoselachogaleokranioleipsanodrim hypotrimmatosilphioparaomelitokatakechy-menokichlepikossyphophattoperisteralektry-onoptekephalliokigklopeleiolagoiosiraiobaphe traganopterygon?"

"Just a lucky guess," Totz said.

"Come quickly," Rasher said. "I'm in the middle of an experiment."

Rasher led them along the twisty hallways to his lab. Pipes and wires crisscrossed in every direction. Workbenches were cluttered with all sorts of tools and equipment. In the center of the room stood a bed. On it lay a turkey leg wrapped in clear plastic.

"What are you working on?" Totz asked.

"Have you ever wondered why some foods stay fresh for a long time and other foods quickly grow stale?" Rasher asked.

"Nope," Slice said. "I'm always fresh!"

"I'm working on a way to keep food at peak freshness," Rasher said. "I call it the Stay-Fresh-o-Lator. Stay fresh with Stay-Fresh-o-Lator!"

The turkey leg tried to say something from under the plastic, but his voice was muffled.

"Can he breathe under there?" Fry asked.

"Food loves being in plastic," Rasher declared. "It keeps us young."

THE STAY-FRESH-O-LATOR IS LIKE A DAY AT THE SPA!

The turkey leg nodded and gave a thumbs-up.

"So, why the visit?" Rasher asked. "I'm

guessing you're not looking for a few hours in the Stay-Fresh-o-Lator."

"We need your help," Scoop said. She explained everything that had happened—the visit from the Mobile Donut Command Center, what happened to Strawberry Surprise in Sub-Basement 3, and how Cruller Team 7 got wiped out by Mus Musculus.

"Mus Musculus," Rasher said, "interesting."

"Do you know anything about the Sub-Basements of the school?" Totz asked.

Rasher thought a moment. "I only know that Sub-Basement 1 is where the Tools of Belching Walrus Elementary live. Their leader is Drillbit Magoo. A zany fellow, doesn't get out much. He likes to put holes in things."

Slice, Scoop, Totz, and Fry looked at one another in concern.

"What's in Sub-Basements 2 and 3?" Scoop asked.

"I only know that those who dare to go that deep into the Sub-Basements never return," Rasher said. "And those who never heard of the Sub-Basements live longer, happier lives."

"Mus Musculus said he is going to cut the power to the school if we don't give him all our cheese and crackers," Slice said.

"Great goulash! Some of my closest friends are crackers!" Rasher said.

"Maybe you could give us a few gadgets that will help us," Totz said.

Rasher wiped the bacon grease from his forehead and thought a moment. "It is difficult when I don't know what's down there, but maybe I can find a few things for you."

Rasher dug through piles of junk and pulled out a black backpack. He handed it to Scoop. "I call this a Cryo-Matic-Suit-o-Lator. I've heard it can get very hot in the Sub-Basements. The Cryo-Matic-Suit-o-Lator will help keep you at the perfect temperature."

"This is amazing," Scoop said. "Thank you."

"Be careful," Rasher said. "It only works for a few minutes."

"That's great," Slice said. "Now Scoop can come with us anywhere."

"Slice!" Rasher said. "I have something for you, too."

Rasher pressed a button, and a panel opened on the wall. Inside sat three small red-and-white balls.

"I call these Peppermint-o-Lators," Rasher said. "If you ever need to make a quick escape, throw a Peppermint-o-Lator, and it will make a puff of white smoke. It will also make your breath minty fresh."

"I love minty-fresh breath," Slice said.

"And, Totz," Rasher said. "It's time to upgrade your headphones."

"But I like my headphones," Totz said.

Rasher pulled out what looked like an ordinary set of headphones. He pressed a button on it, and a grappling hook and rope shot out.

"Whoa," they all said.

Rasher dug around his messy bench some more. "And for all of you, I have these . . ." He held out four pairs of sunglasses.

"Thank you, but I already have a pair of sunglasses," Totz said.

"Press the button on the right side," Rasher said.

They put on the sunglasses and pressed the button. Everything turned green, but they could see very clearly.

"It's like I can see twice as well," Slice said.

"I call them Sunglasses-o-Lators," Rasher said. "Not only will they help you see the

tiniest details, but they will help you see in the dark."

"Thanks so much," Slice said to Rasher. "I'm sure these will come in handy."

"And, of course, there's this . . ." Rasher dug through the items on his bench some more. He tossed aside parts and unfinished gadgets. Finally, he pulled out a small bundle. "I thought you might like a free sample of Stay-Fresh-o-Lator."

"No, thanks," Totz said. "I think we're fresh enough."

But Fry took the bundle of folded plastic. "I'll stay fresh with Stay-Fresh-o-Lator."

"Very good!" Rasher said. "Now, you all be careful down there. Like I said before, the Sub-Basement of Belching Walrus Elementary is no joke."

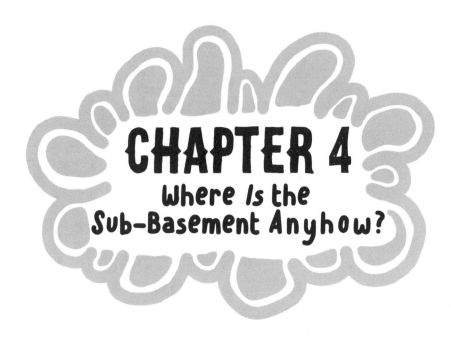

CHAPTER 4
Where *Is* the Sub-Basement Anyhow?

Where is this Sub-Basement anyhow?" Fry asked as they walked down the Hallway.

"Glizzy told me Spex from the Library might know," Scoop said.

Totz tucked his notepad into his pocket. "Food is not allowed in the Library," he said. "They'll chase us right out."

"Or send us into the Maze of Shelves,"

Slice said. "Someone could get lost in there!"

"We'll need a plan," Scoop said.

"I have an idea," Fry said. "Let's send in Cruller Team 8 to take over the Library. Then they'll have to tell us."

"That's no way to be a spy," Totz said. "I stopped by the Art Room for some supplies. Time to put my spy skills to the test."

KNOCK KNOCK KNOCK!!!

The door to the Library swung open, and in walked what looked to be a huge red book.

"Hello," the book said in a voice as deep as Totz could make. "My name is Rimes the rhyming dictionary. If you give me a word, I can tell you all the words that rhyme with it."

Spex ran over. Richard the dictionary followed close behind.

"We've been waiting for you for a long time

now," Spex said. "Welcome to the Library."

"Thank you," Rimes said. "It was a long trip."

"I'm sure it was," Spex said. She led them past the desk and into the Maze of Shelves. They turned left past the Mystery Section.

Since Slice, Scoop, and Fry couldn't see, and they didn't know what direction to walk or how fast to go. Totz tried his best to steer them with his feet: a shake of the left foot meant to go left, a shake of the right foot meant to go right. But they still kept bumping into shelves, the wall, the rolling chair, or Spex and Richard.

"You're a clumsy one, aren't you?" Spex said, turning after the Chapter Book Section.

"I'll be better once I have a chance to rest," Totz said. "By the way, do you have a map that will show us where the door to the Sub-Basement is?"

Spex paused. "That's an unusual question."

"I'm just interested in Sub-Basement doors," Totz said. "Sub-Basement doors are the best."

Richard looked at Rimes suspiciously.

"Here we are," Spex said. "The Reference Section. You'll be staying right next to Richard. Isn't that exciting, Richard? You have a new neighbor."

Richard narrowed his eyes at Rimes. "Something is odd," he said.

"Balderdash," Spex said. "You're just upset that you'll have to share your shelf."

Richard looked Rimes up and down. Rimes took a small, wobbly step back.

"Should we run?" Slice whispered.

Totz shook his head. "Not yet," he whispered through clenched teeth.

Richard lumbered closer. "It is strange that Rimes the rhyming dictionary has not said a single rhyme since he's been here."

"I can rhyme," Rimes said.

"Then I challenge you to a *rhyme-off,*" Richard said. "I will say a sentence, and you give me a sentence that rhymes with it."

"Richard, is this really necessary?" Spex asked.

"I get it," Rimes said to Richard. "You want to make sure your new rhyming dictionary is the best out there. I'm not afraid of a challenge. Bring it on."

Richard smiled.

"But if I prove myself," Rimes said. "You'll tell me where the door to the Sub-Basement is hidden?"

Richard nodded. "It's a deal."

"Totz will be good at this," Scoop whispered. "He's a rhyming master."

"Even *I've* heard of his skills," Fry whispered back.

"Sounds *easy,* and *breezy,* and doesn't make

me *queasy*," Rimes said. "Can I get a beat?"

Suddenly, books started opening and shutting to a slow beat.

Boom. Tap . . . Boom-boom-tap . . . Boom. Tap . . . Boom-boom-tap!

Richard began: *"Hanging out on the shelves at Belching Walrus . . ."*

Without a pause, Rimes jumped in: *"Just me, an atlas, a cookbook, and thesaurus."*

"Sit quiet in the day, but busy all night . . ." Richard said.

"Lounging 'round, all profound, till the break of daylight," Rimes answered back.

Richard looked slightly impressed. *"Spex is the leader, with her buddy Richard."*

Richard wasn't an easy word to rhyme, so Rimes missed a beat. *"Uh . . . Not a bad scene, all things considered."*

Richard stared at Rimes. Rimes stared back. The beat thumped, and Richard went on: *"Some books are blue, and some are orange . . ."*

Rimes said: *"Orange, orange, orange, orange, orange, orange, orange."*

The beat stopped.

Spex gasped.

Slice, Scoop, and Fry tensed.

"Do we run now?" Slice whispered.

Totz squeezed Slice's crust to tell him to wait.

"What kind of rhyming dictionary cannot rhyme a simple word like *orange?*" Spex asked. "I'm disappointed."

"It's a trick," Totz said. "There are no words that rhyme with *orange.*"

Richard lumbered closer. "He's right. I tried to trick him," he said. "I tried to trick him, and he *passed!*"

Books on the shelves cheered.

Slice, Scoop, and Fry breathed sighs of relief.

"I'd be glad to share my shelf with Rimes," Richard said.

"And the map to the Sub-Basement?" Rimes asked.

"Of course," Spex said. "It's right in the

School Archive."

"*Take five,*" Rimes said. "We're going to take a *nose dive* when we *arrive* in the *archive.*"

"Now that's the rhyming I like to hear!" Spex said.

Spex led them out of the Maze of Shelves and across the carpet.

"Have you ever heard of the School Archive?" Slice whispered to Scoop as they walked.

"I've only heard rumors," Scoop said. "It's top secret."

CHAPTER 5

A Sticky Situation

Spex and Richard led them to a glass door behind the checkout desk. Rimes followed, bumping into everything along the way. Spex pressed buttons on a keypad, and a purple light scanned up and down her lenses. The keypad glowed green, and the door swung open.

"Cool," Fry whispered.

"My legs are tired from carrying this big fake book around," Slice whispered.

"Just a little longer," Scoop said.

The walls of the Belching Walrus Elementary School Archive were covered with old photos of the school and the land around it. Shelves and cabinets overflowed with folders, books, and poster tubes.

"It looks like a mess," Spex said, "but the School Archive is the most important part of the Library, maybe the whole school."

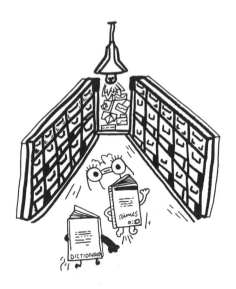

"It holds all the information about Belching Walrus Elementary," Richard added.

Spex clapped her hands, and one of the poster tubes slid from a shelf. It landed on the floor, and the top popped off. Dozens of torn bits of paper floated out.

"What in the world . . . ?" Richard said.

"Compass Rose the map is shredded!" Spex said.

"What *matters* is that *tatters* have *scattered*," Rimes said.

Fry peered out between the folds of red construction paper. "I can fix that," he whispered.

"Shhh," Slice said.

"But I'm a medic," Fry said. "I can help."

Fry slid out of the costume. Rimes began to topple over, but Scoop and Slice held the disguise up.

"Hello!" Fry said. "My name is Rubby. I may look like a donut, but I'm the newest in eraser technology. Not only can I erase pencil marks, but I can erase pen ink, Magic Marker, and . . . uh . . . paint spills!"

"Eraser technology?" Spex said, peering at Fry suspiciously.

"You can erase paint spills?" Richard asked.

"You didn't get the message from the Main Office?" Fry said.

"I did not," Spex said. "How can we help you?"

"The more important question is how can *I* help *you?*" Fry pushed past Spex and looked at the shreds of paper. "Not only am I the newest in eraser technology, but I can fix this map."

"Impossible," Richard said. "There are dozens of pieces."

"Give me a chance," Fry said. "What do you have to lose?"

"Rubby is right," Rimes said. "Give him a chance."

Fry began arranging the pieces on the floor. "I'll just need some tape," he said.

Spex clapped her hands and a tape dispenser lumbered in.

"You called?" the tape dispenser said.

Fry got busy arranging scraps of paper on the floor. He spun pieces this way and that. He placed them down and moved them around. A few times, he climbed on a chair to inspect his work from above. Before long, Fry had all the edges of the map taped together.

Richard handed Fry a piece of paper. "I can see the Tech Room on this piece."

"And the Science Room," Spex said. "The Science Room goes over there."

Once Spex and Richard started helping, the work went quickly. Soon, the whole map was in one piece and they could see all of Belching Walrus Elementary spread before them.

"He's an *ape* with the *tape*. Get this hero a

cape," Rimes said. "Or a *crepe*."

Suddenly, the map spoke. "Thank you!" Compass Rose said. "Do you know what it's like being a mess of tattered pieces? One minute you're a perfectly healthy and crisp map—accurate to the smallest detail. The next, you're stuffed into a tube and forgotten."

"What happened?" Rimes asked.

"I'm not sure," Compass Rose said. "It was dark. I was minding my own business, making sure every water fountain in Belching Walrus Elementary was in the right place. The next thing I knew, someone tackles me and gnaws me to shreds!"

Spex studied the map. "If this map is correct . . ."

"Ahem," Compass Rose said, slightly insulted.

"Of course, this map is correct," Spex said. "According to Compass Rose, the door to the Sub-Basement is between the doors to the Gym and the Art Room."

"Funny," Rimes said. "I've been past the Gym a hundred times. I've never seen a door to the Sub-Basement there before."

"Doors to Sub-Basements are not supposed to be noticed," Spex said. "They're supposed to blend in."

By now, Slice's legs were burning and began to give way. Rimes began to wobble.

"You told us you were new to Belching

Walrus Elementary," Richard said. "Now you're saying you've been past the Gym a hundred times . . ."

"I said that?" Rimes said. "You must be mistaken."

"I'm a dictionary," Richard said. "I never forget a word."

Suddenly, Slice's knees bent and he fell. Scoop slipped the other way. Totz fell off Slice's back, and Rimes came tumbling down. Torn construction paper flew in every direction, and they all landed in a heap at Richard's feet.

"Slice . . . Scoop . . . Totz . . ." Spex   said. "Food . . . in the Library. Food is not permitted in the Library . . . SEIZE THEM!"

Slice wasn't sure what the word *seize* meant, but the way Spex said it, he knew he did not want to be seized.

"Run!" he yelled.

Slice, Scoop, Totz, and Fry ran.

CHAPTER 6

To the Sub-Basement We Go!

Slice, Scoop, Totz, and Fry burst out of the School Archive. They ran across the Library and out into the Hallway. After a few quick turns, a shortcut through the Auditorium, and several minutes inside an air-conditioning vent, the coast looked clear.

"I'd say that was a successful spy activity," Totz said.

"That was *not* successful!" Slice said. "We got caught!"

"It would have been better if they never knew," Totz said. "But we got the information we need and we're all safe. Spy mission successful."

"He's right," Fry said. "A mission is successful if you get the information you need."

"Shhh," Scoop said. "They're coming."

They peered through the vent. Richard, a date stamper, and a team of Magic Markers ran past calling to one another.

"They're not in the Gym!"

"The Nurse's Office is clear!"

"Hallway 4B is empty!"

When the coast was clear again, Slice, Scoop, Totz, and Fry climbed out of the vent and tiptoed down the next hallway.

"Compass Rose said the door to the Sub-Basement is between the Art Room and the Gym," Totz said.

When they got to the end of the hallway, they crept past a tall ladder. A gray door

loomed above them. The door was covered with scratches. The hinges were rusty.

Fry worked his tiny hands around the edge of the door and pulled.

It didn't budge.

Soon, Slice, Scoop, and Totz pulled, too.

"It's not opening," Slice grunted.

"Maybe the door is rusted shut," Scoop said. "I wish Rasher had given us some oil."

"That's it," Totz said. "Help me push that ladder next to the door."

Slice, Scoop, and Fry rushed to the ladder and slid it closer to the door. Totz climbed to the first hinge. He rubbed his hands together and squeezed his fists as tight as he could. He strained and squeezed some more.

"What are you doing?" Scoop called up to him.

"Don't hurt yourself," Slice said.

"He's making oil," Fry said in wonder.

Totz strained again, and a single drop of oil dropped from his fist. It landed on the hinge.

"Now the top hinge," Totz said.

He climbed a few rungs and did the same

as before. Another drop of oil fell onto the other hinge.

Slice pulled on the door, and it swung open without a squeak.

"Resourcefulness!" Fry said. "That's another spy skill!"

RESOURCEFULNESS IS BEING ABLE TO FIND QUICK, CLEVER WAYS TO SOLVE PROBLEMS.

The stairs down to Sub-Basement 1 were dark. Cobwebs hung from the ceiling. The steps creaked. Although a cool breeze blew, somehow it felt hot. Slice's cheese got a little melty.

At the bottom of the stairs, they saw light coming from the far corner. Two figures sat hunched over a small table. One was a hammer, and the other was a screwdriver.

"Do you have any threes?" the hammer asked.

"Go fish," said the screwdriver.

When they saw Slice, Scoop, Totz, and Fry approaching, they dropped their cards.

"Halt!" the hammer said.

"Who goes there?" the screwdriver said.

"My name is Slice," Slice said. "These are my friends Scoop, Totz, and Fry."

The hammer's eyes widened. "Wait, you're *the* Slice?"

Slice's sauce reddened just a bit. "I am," he said proudly.

"Never heard of you," the hammer said. "Now, go back upstairs before some-one gets hurt."

"Or eaten," the screwdriver said.

The two laughed and went back to their cards.

"We need to rescue our friends," Scoop said. "They were attacked by someone named Mus Musculus, and—"

"Did you say Mus Musculus?" the screwdriver asked.

"We did," Totz said. "And we need to solve this problem by midnight."

"We *have* heard of Mus Musculus," the hammer said. "My name is Slammy, and this is Twisty. Come with us."

They followed Slammy and Twisty through a door into another room.

Tools of all shapes and sizes were discussing something that sounded very important.

Slammy and Twisty pulled someone aside and whispered in their ear. An electric drill spun toward them and walked over.

"My name is Drillbit Magoo," the drill said. "Slammy and Twisty tell me you're here to stop Mus Musculus."

"The residents of the Cafeteria are in great danger," Scoop said.

DRILLBIT
MAGOO

"The Cafeteria, you say?" Drillbit said. "I've been to the Cafeteria
many times. I hung the bulletin boards.
I put in the outlets behind the Cooler. I
posted the recycling signs and the signs that say
STACK YOUR TRAYS."

TAKE WHAT
YOU WANT.
BUT EAT WHAT
YOU TAKE

Drillbit looked down at his feet. "But I haven't been on a job in a long time."

"What happened?" Slice asked.

Drillbit spun around. "*This* is what happened."

The crowd gasped.

"My cord was cut," Drillbit explained. "It's one of the worst things that can happen to a power tool."

"Oh, it's terrible!" a saw said. "Forever useless!"

Fry looked closely at Drillbit's injury. "It's a serious cut," he said. "Straight through the power cord. Frayed around the edges, almost like someone chewed through it."

"Like someone *chewed* through it?" Totz said.

"It was Mus Musculus!" Drillbit said. "He's coming for all of us! Before you know it, he'll cut every cord in Sub-Basement 1, and we'll all end up in the Great Dumpster!"

Tools began to flail their arms around and wail.

"Don't worry," Fry said. "I can fix this."

"It's hopeless," Drillbit said. "They're already talking about getting a cordless drill.

Battery packs are the future."

"It's never hopeless," Fry said.

"You should see how Fry patched up Compass Rose in the Library," Scoop added. "He's a natural!"

"I'll need a wire stripper, a wire nut, some wooden dowels, and electrical tape," Fry said.

A tool that looked like a pair of scissors with small notches in its blade hopped forward. "Splice at your service!" she said. "And I have a wire nut right here."

A black roll of electrical tape rolled out of the crowd. "I'd gladly go to any length to help Drillbit Magoo!"

Fry went to work. First, he had Splice clean the frayed wire by removing a short piece of the rubber. A length of shiny copper glinted. Next, Fry paired Drillbit's stub with the end of the cut cord and twisted Wire Nut onto the two ends. Then he took a length of black electrical tape and wrapped it around everything.

Fry inspected his handiwork and made one last adjustment. "Good as new," he said.

Drillbit's plug snaked across the floor and slid into an outlet.

Zip, zip, zip!

Drillbit's drill bit spun. "How can I ever repay you?" he asked.

"Can I keep those wooden dowels?" Fry asked. "They may come in handy."

"You can have as many wooden dowels as you like!" Drillbit said.

Slice stepped forward. "You can also show us how to get to Sub-Basement 2."

Drillbit Magoo went pale. "No one goes to Sub-Basement 2," he said.

"We're not no one," Fry said. "We're Carb Team 1."

"Carb Team 1?" Scoop asked him.

"We're all made of carbs," Fry said, shrugging. "It sounded good to me."

Drillbit stepped closer and spoke in a low voice. "Well, Carb Team 1, if you're going to Sub-Basement 2, prepare to get crispy."

CHAPTER 7

If You Can't Stand the Heat . . .

Drillbit led Slice, Scoop, Totz, and Fry under some old school desks to the far end of Sub-Basement 1. "Sub-Basement 2 is a scary

place," he explained. "The *good* news is that Furnacia likes to sleep at night. If you're quiet, you might slip past with no problem."

"Is there *bad* news?" Totz asked.

Drillbit nodded. "Furnacia is huge, bigger than any creature you've ever seen."

Slice gulped.

"She also likes to move around, so you'll never know where she's hiding," Drillbit warned.

Totz and Fry gulped.

"And it can get hot down there, like *really* hot," Drillbit said.

Scoop gulped.

The door to Sub-Basement 2 was smaller than the door between the Art Room and the Gym. It swung open easily, and a hot breeze blew up from the darkness.

"This is as far as I can take you," Drillbit

said. "Now that my cord has been fixed, I have to catch up on my work. Shelves don't hang themselves, you know."

They looked down the stairs. An orange glow flickered.

A drip of melted ice cream trickled down Scoop's cheek. "I think it's time to use my Cryo-Matic-Suit-o-Lator," she said.

Scoop opened her backpack and unfolded the Cryo-Matic-Suit-o-Lator. She pulled the suit over her body and popped her arms into the sleeves. When she placed the helmet

over her head, blue and green lights blinked and a puff of cold air blew on her face.

"This is one way to keep your cool," Scoop said.

"We should hurry," Totz said. "Rasher told us the suit has a short battery life."

Slice, Scoop, Totz, and Fry climbed down the stairs to Sub-Basement 2.

Although Scoop felt nice and chilly, Slice's crust started getting crispy around the edges. "Let's find that door to Sub-Basement 3," he whispered. "And let's hope Furnacia stays asleep."

The halls of Sub-Basement 2 seemed to rumble and glow orange.

"Which way do we go?" Totz said. "It's all so creepy."

"IT IS NOT CREEPY," a voice bellowed. "IT IS MY HOME!"

A blast of fire flared down the hallway. Totz and Fry dove to one side. Slice and Scoop dodged the other way.

"Run!" Slice called out.

Carb Team 1 ran.

A second blast flared behind them. They hid behind a metal bin as the flames raged past.

"THERE IS NO ESCAPE," the voice said.

Scoop looked around and saw a handle on the wall. She pulled it. A small metal door

swung open to reveal a chute that led up.

Another blast of fire rolled down the hall-way. This blast was hotter than the last.

"Let's go," Scoop said.

"But that chute leads *up*," Totz said. "We need to go *down*."

"We don't have a choice," Scoop said. "If we stay here, we're fried."

They scrambled up the chute, their feet slipping on the smooth metal. When they reached the top, they swung another door

open. A dumpster stood in front of them. Garbage spilled over the top. Stinky liquid oozed through cracks in its sides.

"Gross," Slice said, holding his nose.

"It smells like that time Cabbage and Ground Beef fell behind the counter," Slice said.

"No one found them for days," Slice added.

The night sky sparkled above them. Scoop pressed a button on her Cryo-Matic-Suit-o-Lator and the helmet opened. "Totz," she said.

"Climb down to the dumpster and . . ."

But Totz wasn't there. Neither was Fry.

"Where did they go?" Scoop asked.

Slice and Scoop looked down the chute. An orange glow flickered.

"Totz? Fry?" Slice called down the chute hopefully.

No answer.

Scoop put her helmet back on. "We have to save them," she said.

Slice and Scoop both slid back down the chute.

The hallway was quiet.

No blasts of fire. No booming voice.

"Totz . . . Fry . . ." Slice whispered.

Slice and Scoop inched down the hallway. They came to a large room. Chains, wires, and cobwebs hung from the ceiling. The only light came from the far corner. It was a small orange

flicker no brighter than a birthday candle.

"Totz . . . Fry . . ." Scoop whispered.

"Over here," Fry called out. "It's okay."

When they got there, Totz and Fry were a little more baked than usual. A huge, rusty furnace breathed smoke behind them.

"This is our new friend Furnacia," Totz said. "Fry helped her out."

"She had a leak," Fry said. "I patched her up with some scrap metal and duct tape. I also changed her filter and cleaned her vents."

"I DON'T KNOW HOW TO THANK YOU," Furnacia said. "I WAS LOSING SO MUCH HEAT, IT WAS HARD TO KEEP THE SCHOOL WARM."

"It's what a medic does," Fry said.

"That's amazing!" Scoop said.

"It really was," Totz said. "Furnacia told us about her problem and Fry snapped right into action."

"FRY THE MEDIC," Furnacia said, "YOU AND YOUR FRIENDS ARE

ALWAYS WELCOME IN SUB-BASEMENT 2. PLEASE LET ME KNOW IF THERE IS ANYTHING I CAN DO TO HELP YOU."

"Maybe you help us stop Mus Musculus?" Slice asked. "He wants all our cheese and crackers by midnight or he will invade the Cafeteria."

"I HAVE MY OWN PROBLEMS WITH MUS MUSCULUS," Furnacia said. "HE AND F.E.A.R.S.O.M.E. HAVE TAKEN ALL MY COAL. WITHOUT MY COAL, I'M NOTHING MORE THAN A COLD METAL BOX."

"Who *is* Mus Musculus?" Slice asked. "And why would he want your coal?"

"I'VE NEVER SEEN HIM," Furnacia said. "BUT THEY NEED TO COME THROUGH SUB-BASEMENT 2 TO GET TO THE CAFETERIA. WHEN I'M FILLED WITH COAL, IT'S TOO HOT FOR THEM."

Furnacia pointed to the empty metal bins. "NOW THAT MY COAL IS NEARLY GONE, THEY CAN GO ANYWHERE THEY LIKE. I'VE LET YOU DOWN. I'VE LET THE CAFETERIA DOWN. I'VE LET DOWN ALL OF BELCHING WALRUS ELEMENTARY."

"We've got less than an hour," Fry said, "but Carb Team 1 will stop Mus Musculus, F.E.A.R.S.O.M.E., and their plans to take over the school."

The trouble was that Fry sounded way more confident than anyone on Carb Team 1 felt. This wasn't going to be easy.

CHAPTER 8
Into the Secret Lair

Furnacia moved aside and showed them the door to Sub-Basement 3. It was an old piece of rotting wood held together by rusty nails. The door creaked open, and Slice, Scoop, Totz, and Fry went down. A cool breeze blew up the stairs, and Scoop could take off her Cryo-Matic-Suit-o-Lator.

"Just in time," Scoop said. "The suit is out of power."

"Furnacia could get a job in the Cafeteria making coal-fired pizza," Slice said. "She's hot."

Totz admired his new crispiness. "I kind of liked it," he said.

At the bottom of the stairs, they came to a metal door. A red light blinked below a screen that showed eight squares. Each square had a letter in it:

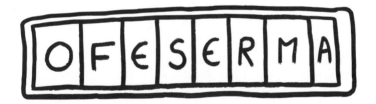

"What does it say?" Slice asked.

"It says *OFESERMA*," Totz said.

"What does *OFESERMA* mean?" Slice said.

"It doesn't mean anything," Scoop said, looking closely at the screen. "To open this door, we're going to have to get the right combination of letters."

"There have to be a million combinations of those letters," Slice said.

ACTUALLY, THERE ARE 40,320 COMBINATIONS OF THOSE LETTERS.

Slice pushed a bunch of letters, hoping to get it right. *EMOFARSE.*

A red light buzzed, and another metal door slammed shut behind them.

"We're trapped!" Scoop said.

The room suddenly got colder, and a shrill

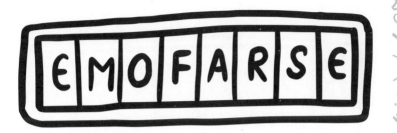

voice sounded. It was Mus Musculus.

"Ah, our heroes have come to save the day," he said. "Unless you've brought our cheese and crackers, I'm afraid you'll be standing in the cold."

"Carb Team 1 is coming to stop you!" Fry called out.

Totz pressed another combination of letters: *ROMAFESE.*

The red light buzzed, and it got colder still.

"ROMAFESE?" Mus Musculus laughed. "That's not even a word! Now, be careful. Every time you get a wrong answer, it will get colder."

Fry pushed some buttons. *EARSOFME.*

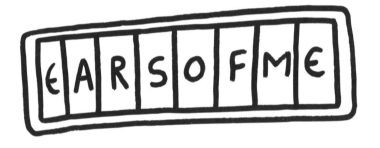

The red light buzzed again, and it became even colder. They could see their breath in the air.

"Stop pushing buttons," Scoop said. "We need to think."

"I *was* thinking," Fry said. "It spells *EARS OF ME.*"

"Spelling . . ." Totz said. "That's it. What other words can we spell with those letters?"

He rubbed his hands together and pressed letters. *MORE SAFE.*

The red light buzzed. The temperature dropped again.

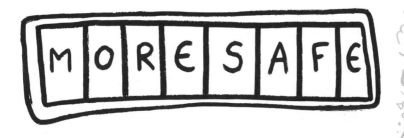

"*MORE SAFE?*" Mus Musculus laughed. "It seems to me you're *less safe.* Now, I must go. It is almost midnight. Goodbye, Carb Team 1."

At this point, Slice, Totz, and Fry were nearly frozen. Frost covered their faces.

"Sc-Sc-Sc-Scoop . . . Tr-try . . . Ag-g-g-ain . . ." Slice said, shivering.

Even for an ice cream cone, it was getting too cold in the freezer trap. Ice crystals swirled as Scoop trudged through the frost.

What could those letters spell? Scoop thought.

Then she saw it. It seemed so obvious now!

She pressed the buttons. *FEARSOME.*

A green light went on, and the door in front of them opened. Scoop rushed to her friends.

"Are you okay?" she asked.

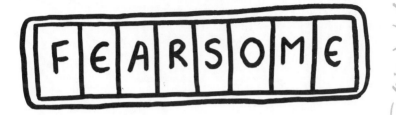

"Who hasn't had a little freezer burn?" Totz said, standing up.

"I feel fresher than ever," Fry said.

WHO DOESN'T LOVE FROZEN PIZZA??

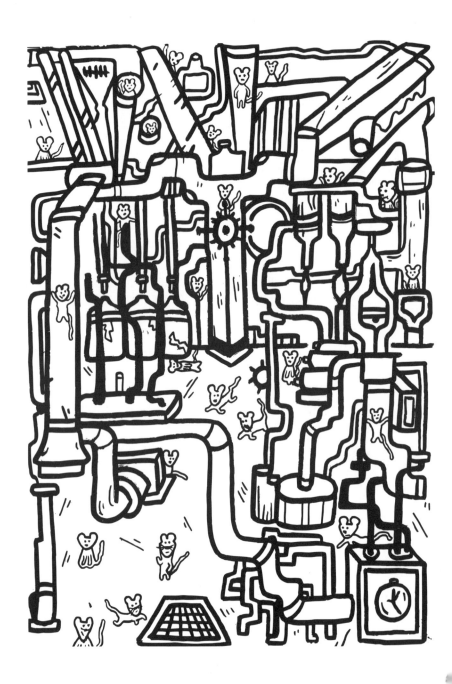

They walked on. Bright lights lit the perfectly white hallway. Ahead of them, they heard computers beeping and machinery whirring. When they turned the corner, they saw it.

The Mechanical Room was huge. Clusters of wires snaked in every direction, and shiny green pipes turned this way and that. A row of light blue boiler tanks hummed. In one corner, an army of mice of all colors and sizes was working hard at something. Nearby,

MUS MUSCULUS

one single mouse, the largest of them all, sat in an overturned hard hat as though it was a throne.

"Keep at it!" the large mouse hollered. "We only have twenty minutes."

"That must be Mus Musculus," Slice said.

"He's huge," Fry said.

"One huge mouse isn't as bad as a hundred tiny mice," Totz said.

"We've got both," Scoop said.

"Look there," Fry said. He pointed to the farthest corner of the room.

"It's an upside-down milk crate," Slice

100 MICE = 1,800 TEETH + 1,800 CLAWS!

said. "We have about a hundred of them in the Cafeteria."

"But look *under* the milk crate," Fry said.

Slice looked closer. Cruller Team 7 huddled with Strawberry Surprise. They all had bites taken out of them.

Slice thought about all his friends in the Cafeteria. He thought about Glizzy and Sprinkles. He thought about Sal and Monella. Then he thought about the rest of the school—the Art Room, the Main Office, the Tech Room.

Everyone needed the power supply. This was the greatest danger Belching Walrus Elementary had ever faced.

"We've got to stop Mus Musculus," Slice said.

"But Strawberry Surprise . . . Cruller Team 7," Fry said. "We've got to save them."

"We've got to do both," Scoop said. "It looks like it's time to split up."

Slice knew mice meant great danger. Food told their children tales of mice nibbling at them if they didn't do their chores. Around campfires, food whispered about mice to frighten young campers. No food wanted to come face-to-face with a mouse. Ever.

But what choice did they have?

"Let's do this," Slice said.

CHAPTER 9
Time to Split Up

Carb Team la:

Slice and Totz crept through the Mechanical Room toward the mice. They hid behind every post and piece of equipment they could find.

:SNEAK:

"This is a bad idea," Slice said. "We're going to be eaten to crumbs."

"Shh," Totz warned.

"We need to be as quiet as a cat."

"What's a cat?" Slice asked.

"You know," Totz said. "Furry with pointy ears. Long whiskers and a tail. Very quiet."

"Well, whatever it is, I'm sure a cat wouldn't be foolish enough to mess with a mouse," Slice said.

They hid behind an electrical box and peeked around the edge. The mice were feverishly gnawing at a cluster of cables. Teeth chewed. Claws sliced.

"Keep at it," Mus Musculus said. "Once we cut the power, all the food in the Cafeteria

will be ours for the eating. All the construction paper in the Art Room will be ours for the nesting. All the trombones in the Music Room will be ours for the playing!"

One of the worker mice lifted his head. "You play the trombone?" he squeaked.

"You don't seem like the musical type," another mouse said.

"I don't play the trombone," Mus Musculus said. "But once we take over Belching Walrus Elementary, I could *learn* to play the trombone!"

"Why can't you learn now?" another mouse said.

"Just keep chewing!" Mus Musculus barked.

Totz stepped back and tripped over a pile of rags. There were a bunch of pipe cleaners and a few loose wires as well.

"You saw what they did to Strawberry Surprise and Cruller Team 7," Slice said, helping Totz to his feet. "Are we supposed to just go over there and ask them to stop chewing on the cable?"

Totz looked at the pile he had just tripped over. He had an idea.

"That's exactly what we're going to do," Totz said.

Carb Team 1b:

Scoop and Fry crept down the stairs. Before

long, they were making their way across the shiny floor to the overturned milk crate.

"I hope Strawberry Surprise is okay," Fry said. "When I was just a tiny lump of dough, she taught me how to do a tornado kick."

"That sounds very advanced," Scoop said.

"I'm a natural when it comes to self-defense," Fry said. "It's one of the reasons my father wants me to take over as Captain Donut. But just because you're good at something shouldn't mean you have to spend your life doing it."

They tiptoed along the wall past a bunch of pipes.

"Why don't you *want* to take over as Captain Donut?" Slice asked. "Running the Mobile Donut Command Center sounds like an important job."

"Being a medic is an important job, too," Fry said. "Plus, it makes me feel good."

"I get it," Scoop said. "If someone tried to stop me from painting, I don't know what I'd do."

They crept around a generator and found themselves behind the overturned milk crate.

COME ON!

"Hey," Fry whispered to the donuts. "This is my friend Scoop. We're here to save you."

"It's no use, Fry," one of the donuts said. He was a long, glazed cruller with green sprinkles. "We can't move the milk crate."

"Anyhow, look at us," Strawberry Surprise said. "We're half eaten."

"You're not half eaten," Fry said. "You're half *un*-eaten. Now, help me in there."

"What could you possibly do?" another nibbled Cruller asked. "It's only a matter of time before the Mice get hungry and finish us off."

Fry squeezed himself between the bars of the milk crate.

"You were right," Scoop said to Fry. "Sometimes little *can* be good."

"Hand me the Stay-Fresh-o-Lator wrap and the wooden dowels," Fry said. "I have an idea."

"I have no idea what sort of idea you have," Scoop said, "but any idea is better than no idea."

She pushed the supplies between the bars.

Carb Team 1a:

"I don't even know what a cat *is*," Slice said.

"Be quiet and walk forward," Totz said. "Tell the mice to stop or you'll pounce on them."

"Cats can pounce?"

"Yes."

"What's my name?" Slice asked.

"Make one up," Totz hissed.

Slice wobbled forward.

Mus Musculus looked at them. Several mice stopped chewing and looked at them as well.

"My name is Mr. Puffles," Slice said. "I'm a cat . . . er . . . Now, stop chewing on those power cables."

More mice stopped chewing and looked up. A few started backing away.

"Ah, a cat," Mus Musculus said. "A bit of a surprise, but not unexpected."

Mus Musculus climbed out of his hard hat and paced across the floor. He looked Mr. Puffles up and down. "You wouldn't be the first cat I've stopped. I'm sure you've heard of the famous Persians named Milo and Luna . . . ?"

"Er . . . no," Mr. Puffles said.

"What about the mighty ragdoll named Snowball?" Mus Musculus said. "She put up a great fight, but I am still here."

"I've never heard of Snowball, either," Mr. Puffles said. "But they are nothing compared to the unstoppable Mr. Puffles!"

"I'm afraid you're wrong."

Mus Musculus snapped his fingers. A team of mice scurried out holding a large pen.

"You see, cats may be silent and strong," Mus Musculus said. "They may be fierce hunters of mice. They may even be bigger than mice and have sharper claws. But cats have one weakness."

"Uh-oh," Totz said. He peeked out from under the rags.

Mus Musculus snapped his fingers, and the mice pressed a button on the pen. A beam of light shot out and made a bright red dot on the floor in front of Mr. Puffles.

"I've heard of this," Totz whispered. "You have to chase the dot."

"That's silly," Slice whispered back. "I'm not chasing that dot."

"Cats can't help themselves," Totz said. "You have to."

Slice sighed and began chasing the dot. Totz did his best to keep up, but it wasn't easy under the rags.

Mr. Puffles darted left. Mr. Puffles darted right. Mr. Puffles zigzagged. Wherever the dot moved, Slice struggled to catch it. He stomped at the dot. He swatted at the dot, but each time it slipped away.

"Faster," Totz said. "You have to be cat-like."

"I don't even know what a cat *is*," Slice said.

Finally, Slice saw the bright red dot on the wall in front of him. He leaped at it and smashed against the bricks.

Mus Musculus walked over.

"More food," Mus Musculus said, stroking his whiskers. "Excellent."

He turned to the mice. "Tie them up and keep chewing," he said. "Within moments, we will control all of Belching Walrus Elementary!"

CHAPTER 10

Spies vs. Villains

Slice could see the mice were almost through the power cable, so he tried to stall them.

"So, what does F.E.A.R.S.O.M.E. stand for anyway?" he asked.

"It stands for <u>F</u>ood <u>E</u>ating for <u>A</u>ll <u>R</u>odents, <u>S</u>ome <u>O</u>ctopi, and <u>M</u>any <u>E</u>lephants," Mus Musculus announced.

"That sounds totally random," Totz said.

"There were not enough hungry octopi for them to start their own group," Mus Musculus said, "so they joined ours. Mostly for the health insurance."

"And the elephants?" Slice asked.

THE HEALTH INSURANCE IS VERY GOOD!!

"Okay, the elephants I made up," Mus Musculus said. "But I wanted our organization to spell a word."

"You don't have to do this," Totz said.

"Oh, but I do," Mus Musculus said. "Mice can't show a whisker upstairs. There are traps and all sorts of other dangers, so we live hungry in the darkness. Well, those days are over."

"Maybe we can help you solve your problems," Slice said.

"We've very good at solving problems," Totz added. "Just ask Furnacia. Just ask Drill-bit Magoo."

"All you'll do is give us your scraps," Mus Musculus said. "Mice will still be feared. Mice will still have to hide in the deepest parts of the school. Once we gnaw through that cable, once we cast the school into darkness, we will be able

to come out of hiding. Mice will RULE Belching Walrus Elementary! We'll have all the food we want. We'll have all the construction paper we want. We'll have all the trombones we want!"

With that, the last nibble on the cable sent them all into darkness.

The Cafeteria went dark.

THE COOLER SHUT OFF!!

The Tech Room went dark.

Even the Main Office went dark.

"Now line up and prepare to march!" Mus Musculus announced.

"Single file?" one mouse asked.

"I think we should line up three across," another mouse said.

"Should we go in height order?" the first mouse asked.

"I don't care," Mus Musculus squeaked. "Just start marching!"

Slice and Totz pressed the button on their sunglasses. Everything looked greenish, but at least they could see.

"What should we do?" Slice said. He struggled, but the knots were too tight.

"If I know anything about being a spy, it's that there is always a way out," Totz said. He struggled, too, but the string just cut into his crispy outer crust.

The mice began to march, three across in height order, toward the stairs.

"Stop right there!"

It was Fry. Scoop stood beside him. They

were both wearing their sunglasses, too.

"How adorable," Mus Musculus said. "A tiny donut and an ice cream cone have come to stop us."

The lined-up mice laughed, squeaked, and giggled.

"That's right," Scoop said. "We've come to stop you."

"You and what army?" Mus Musculus said.

Fry snapped his fingers. "*This* army."

Suddenly, an army of pink cake pops dropped from above and landed on the mice. The neat lines of rodents scattered. Claws

swiped. Cake pop sticks swung. Scoop rushed over to untie Slice and Totz while Fry worked on the cut power cable.

"I could fix this if I had my splicing tools," Fry said.

"Where did you find that army of cake pops?" Slice asked, getting to his feet.

Two cake pops flipped past them and tackled a mouse.

"Fry really *is* a brilliant medic," Scoop

said. "Cruller Team 7 and Strawberry Surprise were in bad shape. But with his wooden dowels, Rasher's Stay-Fresh-o-Lator wrap, and Strawberry Surprise's frosting, Fry gave them new life!"

The battle raged. One moment, it looked as though the mice were winning. The next minute, it looked like Carb Team 1 and the Cake Pop Troopers were winning.

"This gives me a great idea for a rhyme!" Totz said, flipping a mouse over his shoulder.

"You think up rhymes in the middle of a battle?" Slice said, dodging a mouse that ran at him.

"I think up rhymes all the time," Totz said. "I think of them when I'm crisping up in the fryer. I think of them when I'm walking in the Pantry. Sometimes I wake up in the morning and there are rhymes already in my head waiting to be written down."

"You're a natural," Fry said, rolling between a mouse's legs.

"*You're* the natural," Scoop said. She spun around and kicked a mouse's feet out from under her. "Look what you did with Strawberry Surprise and Cruller Team 7. You completely changed them."

"Oh, they may look different on the outside, but they're the same on the inside," Fry said.

EVERYONE IS DIFFERENT

They put up a good fight, but there were just too many mice.

"You can't defeat a hundred hungry mice," Mus Musculus squeaked. "We want our stinky food!"

Slice and Scoop looked at each other.

"Stinky food . . ." Scoop said. "Could it be that easy?"

"There's only one way to find out," Slice said. He turned to the Cake Pop Troopers. "RETREAT!!!"

RETREAT!!

The entire group—Carb Team 1 and the Cake Pop Troopers—ran. They sprinted across the Mechanical Room of Sub-Basement 3. They scrambled up the stairs and through the door to Sub-Basement 2. They even scurried between Furnacia's legs. All the while, Mus Musculus and his mouse army chased them.

"They're gaining on us!" Fry said.

"Not if I can help it!" Slice pulled out the Peppermint-o-Lators Rasher had given him. He tossed them over his shoulder.

POOF! POOF! POOF!

Puffs of white peppermint smoke poofed in the hallway.

"Ahh!" Mus Musculus cried. "Mice HATE peppermint!"

The Peppermint-o-Lators didn't stop the mice, but it slowed them down just enough. They twisted around a few turns and finally saw the handle on the wall next to the metal bin. They dove into the coal chute, scrambled up the tunnel, and burst out of Belching Walrus Elementary.

Totz spun around in the air, pulled off his headphones, and shot his grappling hook. It caught on a pipe overhead. Totz, Slice, Scoop, Fry, and a few cake pops grabbed on to the wire. The mice fell into the dumpster below.

Splat, squish, splat-splat, squish!

Carb Team 1 and the Cake Pop Troopers climbed back into the coal chute and looked down at the dumpster. Mice squished through slime and oozing muck. At first, it sounded like they were crying for help, but after a moment, they realized the mice were shouting in glee.

One was doing a happy backstroke through the stinky dumpster slime.

"That . . . is . . . disgusting . . ." Totz said.

"We saw the dumpster when we were running away from Furnacia," Scoop said.

"When Mus Musculus said they wanted food . . ." Slice said.

"And when he said he wanted the stinkiest

cheese we had . . ." Scoop added.

"Well, we put one and one together and led the mice here," Slice said.

"But it's so gross!" Totz said.

"It may be gross to you and me," Scoop said. "But to them, it's perfect."

"Nope," Slice said. "That's straight-up disgusting."

Mus Musculus pulled himself to the edge of the dumpster. Slime dripped down his forehead. "There is enough food down here to last a lifetime," he said. "How can we thank you?"

"For starters, stop threatening everyone at Belching Walrus Elementary," Totz said.

"Done," Mus Musculus said.

"Also, stay hidden," Slice said. "Only come up here at night."

"We like it best at night," Mus Musculus said.

"And make sure Furnacia gets the coal she needs to keep her fire burning," Scoop added.

"Each night when we go to the Great Dumpster, we will bring her coal," Mus Musculus said. "I am a fair and just ruler. It's only right she eats, too."

And with that, Slice, Scoop, Totz, Fry, and all the Cake Pop Troopers headed back to the Cafeteria.

On the way, they stopped at Sub-Basement 2 to speak with Furnacia.

They also stopped in Sub-Basement 1 to see if the Tools could repair the chewed cables.

When they got back to the Cafeteria, all they could do was collapse.

CHAPTER 11

"Rapping" Things Up

They awoke to find Glizzy, Sprinkles, and Captain Donut standing over them. Mus Musculus was there, too. He was no longer covered in slime. In fact, his fur was combed neatly.

Slice stood and helped the rest of Carb Team 1 to their feet.

Sprinkles flung her arms around Fry.

"Don't you ever scare me like that again," she cried. "You could have gotten your dough overcooked!"

Captain Donut knelt down to Fry. "Mus Musculus and the Cake Pop Troopers told us everything that happened, son," he said. "You took control of a bad situation and turned it around. You used your wit, your strength, and your resourcefulness to save us all."

Slice nudged Scoop. "What about us?" he whispered.

Scoop shushed him.

"Mobile Donut Command Center would be proud to name you our next captain," Captain Donut said.

Fry began to say something, but Captain Donut pulled out a tub of frosting.

"But that is not your path," Captain Donut said. He smeared Fry with white frosting and showered him with red sprinkles.

"I officially name you head medic of Mobile Donut Command Center," Captain Donut said. "It would be wrong to stop you from doing what you love."

Fry smiled as big as a tiny donut had ever smiled.

Glizzy shook hands with Slice, Scoop, and Totz. "You three saved us again," he said.

"How can we ever repay you?" Sprinkles asked.

"If Mus Musculus had won, we would all be in hot water," Slice said.

"Are you sure?" Glizzy said. "The Cafeteria, the Gym, the Library, the Tech Room, all of Belching Walrus Elementary . . . we owe you our lives."

"Well, there is one tiny, little thing," Totz said.

"Name it," Glizzy said.

They named it.

Everyone gathered around while Totz

took the stage. Slammy and Twisty started banging out a beat. Scoop began painting, and Sal and Monella tossed colored sprinkles into the air. Hands clapped. Feet stomped. Totz started spitting rhymes.

Did you ever have a thing you know you can do
But everyone around wants to give it the boot?
Keep sailing straight, keep your eye on the prize,
Cuz you can't be cherry if you're blueberry pie.
Say you're a tot, but you want to be a spy,
Or a brave, smart medic, instead of being just a Fry?
You don't need a map, a plan, or a chart,
Just stay on your course while you follow your heart.
You can feel it in your frosting, your sauce, or your
*   crust.*
If you're made out of metal, you can feel it in your
*   rust.*
If you're a hot, smoky furnace from Sub-Basement 2,

148

Check out your chimney—you can feel it in your flue.

So, listen to me now, you'll know I'm right when it's later,

You'll be amazed, I'm an expert prognosticator.

Never let the world tell you what dreams you should follow.

Or you'll be a cannoli with no cream—just plain hollow.

The crowd cheered louder.

Everyone had a great time.

And they partied until dawn.

Curious to know more about your favorite characters from

BAD FOOD?

Turn the page and find out!

Sal

Type: An Egg

Flavor: Eggy protein with a hint of cholesterol, maybe a bit saltier than Monella

Personality: Cheery, organized, energetic

Strengths: Protective of Monella

Weaknesses: Fragile (almost like an egg!)

Wobble Factor: High

Hobbies: Speed walking, but dancing is his secret talent. Shhh . . .

Monella

Type: Also an Egg

Flavor: Also eggy protein with a hint of cholesterol

Personality: Brave but maybe a bit reckless

Strengths: Protective of the Pantry

Weaknesses: Also fragile (almost like an egg!)

Wobble Factor: Even higher

Hobbies: Speed walking

Glizzy

Name: Glizzy

Food Type: Hot dog

Personality: Wise and gruff

Strengths: A born leader, knows a lot from the old days

Weaknesses: Can't go outside—it's too much to bear after becoming a leftover at the Great School Cookout!

Fear: Soggy irritable bowel syndrome, or SBS (if you think you may suffer from SBS, talk to your doctor or pharmacist)

Is a hot dog a sandwich?: A hot dog is *more* than just a sandwich.

Sprinkles

Name: Sprinkles

Food Type: Pink frosted donut with sprinkles

Personality: Sweet and kind

Strengths: Brings folks together

Weaknesses: Worries often and loses a lot of sprinkles

Hobbies: Knitting sweaters anyway (does food need a sweater?)